Aaaah!!!

I was playing ball with a few kids. The ball went into the woods.

We started to look for it.

Suddenly we saw it. It was in the mouth of the meanest-looking dog I had ever seen.

Huge. Big teeth. Big claws. Glaring eyes. SCARY!

"Aaaah!!" yelled one of the kids.

Everyone fled.

Except me. It was my ball.

First Stepping Stone Books you will enjoy:

By Mary Pope Osborne
(The Magic Tree House series)
Dinosaurs Before Dark (#1)
The Knight at Dawn (#2)
Mummies in the Morning (#3)

By Barbara Park
Junie B. Jones and the Stupid Smelly Bus
Junie B. Jones and a Little Monkey Business
Junie B. Jones and Her Big Fat Mouth

By Louis Sachar
Marvin Redpost: Kidnapped at Birth?
Marvin Redpost: Why Pick on Me?
Marvin Redpost: Is He a Girl?

By Marjorie Weinman Sharmat
The Great Genghis Khan Look-Alike Contest

THE GREAT GENGHIS KHAN LOOK-ALIKE CONTEST

by Marjorie Weinman Sharmat

illustrated by Mitchell Rigie

A FIRST STEPPING STONE BOOK

Random House New York

For my grandson, Nathan Lawrence Sharmat, with much love from Grandma —*M.W.S.*

To Amanda, welcome to the world —*M.R.*

 Published in the United States by Random House, Inc., New York, and simultaneously in Canada by Random House of Canada Limited, Toronto.

Library of Congress Cataloging-in-Publication Data
Sharmat, Marjorie Weinman.
The great Genghis Khan look-alike contest /
by Marjorie Weinman Sharmat ; illustrated by Mitchell Rigie.
p. cm.
"A First stepping stone book."
SUMMARY: Fred enters his mean-looking but sweet dog in a Hollywood contest that could lead to a movie contract, fame, and fortune.
ISBN 0-679-85002-3 (pbk.)—ISBN 0-679-95002-8 (lib. bdg.)
[1. Dogs—Fiction. 2. Contests—Fiction.]
I. Rigie, Mitchell, ill. II. Title.
PZ7.S5299Gp 1993 [E]—dc20 93-12970

Manufactured in the United States of America 10 9 8 7 6 5 4 3 2 1

I owe my mother and father $248.10.

$146.90 for food

$45 for shots

$15 for teeth and nails

$15.20 to get rid of fleas

$9 to get out burs from fur

$5 for a license

$3 for a bowl

$4 for a leash

$5 for a collar

I, Fred Shedd, don't need a license or a leash. Or a collar.

I don't have fleas or burs.

What I do have is a dog.

Last summer I didn't owe my parents a cent. Last summer I didn't have a dog.

Then one day I was playing ball with a few kids. The ball went into the woods.

We started to look for it.

Suddenly we saw it. It was in the mouth of the meanest-looking dog I had ever seen.

Huge. Big teeth. Big claws. Glaring eyes. SCARY!!

"Aaaah!!" yelled one of the kids.

Everyone fled.

Except me. It was my ball.

The dog came up to me. The closer he got, the meaner he looked. “Keep it!” I cried. “Keep the ball. It’s all yours.”

The dog sat down. He cocked his head. He wagged his tail. He waited.

He wanted to give me the ball! Did I dare take it from those teeth?

Slowly I reached out. The dog dropped the ball right into my hand! I called to my friends. But they were nowhere in sight.

The dog kept wagging and waiting. He wanted something.

A pat? Did I dare? I reached over. I patted him. And I kept patting him.

He licked my hand. He was one nice dog.

Then one of his ears went up. What did that mean? I guess it meant he was happy.

I said, “Well, thanks for the ball. Now you go home, and I’ll go home.”

The dog followed me home.

My parents took five steps backward when they saw him.

“It’s okay. He’s nice,” I said.

My mother shrugged. “Looks aren’t everything,” she said. And my folks let the dog in.

For the next few weeks I tried to find out who owned him.

I put up ads.

I made phone calls.

I took him door to door.

That was a mistake.

People answered the door. They looked at the dog. They said, “E-e-e-k!” Or “Ugh!” They asked, “Does he bite?”

They didn’t wait for an answer. They just slammed the door shut.

Would you believe that nobody owned him?

Except me.

My mother and father said I could keep him. All I had to do was pay for everything he cost.

This dog cost a lot.

For openers, he needed kibble.

He needed bones.

Then he needed a flea collar.

He needed his teeth cleaned.

He needed his nails clipped.

He kept needing.

"Can I get a job?" I asked my parents one night at supper. "I need money."

"You have a job," my mother said. "School."

"And you take out the garbage," my father said. "We pay you money. It's called an allowance."

"Yeah, but this dog costs more than what you pay me."

My father sighed. "We don't have much money, Son."

I knew that.

The company my father worked for

closed down. Then my mother's company closed down.

My dad found a new job.

My mother was still looking.

I fiddled with my food.

"Maybe the dog can get a job. He doesn't go to school. He doesn't take out the garbage. He's got plenty of spare time."

"Forget it," said my father. "This dog is unemployable."

"Unemployable?" I asked. "What does that mean?"

"It means that nobody will give him a job. He looks too mean."

"What could he do anyway?" my mother asked.

"Well, fetch things. Or keep lonely people company. Or *something*."

"Are you kidding?" said my mother. "People scream when they see him."

"Just forget it," my father said. "His job is to be a dog."

"That's right," said my mother.

She reached down and patted the dog.

He raised an ear.

This dog really liked my parents.

And they really liked him. They weren't afraid of him. They never said E-e-e-k or Ugh. They only said I had to pay for him.

I was out of luck. Nobody was going to pay this dog for being a dog.

There was something this dog needed that didn't cost money.

He needed a name.

"So, have you named him yet?"

My best friend, Pamela Brinkman, kept asking me the same question.

"Not yet," I said. "I'm still thinking."

The dog was sitting with us outside in my yard.

Pamela wasn't afraid of him.

"This is a good dog," I said. "A tail wagger. A hand licker. An ear raiser. He needs the right name."

Pamela smiled. "With his teeth, there's only one name. *Dracula.*"

"Dracula? No, it's too...toothy."

"Fine. I've got a backup name. How about Duz?"

"Duz?"

"Yeah. What's the first thing people ask when they see him? They ask, *'Does he bite?'*"

"So...?"

"So, Duz is short for *Does he bite?*"

"Huh?"

"That's his name!"

Pamela is bossy. But sometimes I obey her. "Okay," I said. "His name is Duz."

Duz raised an ear. He was happy with his new name.

"Give him a bone," Pamela said. "To celebrate."

I got a bone from a box. Sixteen and

one half cents is what a bone costs.

I groaned. “I will never be able to pay my parents what I owe them.”

“Sure you will. Just let me give you the money,” Pamela said.

Pamela’s parents are rich. They buy her stuff. Anything she wants. They take her on trips. Anywhere she wants to go. Pamela kept wanting to pay for Duz.

“I can’t take your money,” I said. “But thanks again.”

Pamela patted Duz. “Okay, then maybe this dog can make money for you,” she said.

“I already thought of that,” I said. “Forget it. People scream when they see him.”

“Yes!” Pamela said. “Yes, yes!!” She hugged Duz. “This dog scares people, right? So you can hire out Duz as a guard dog to scare burglars!”

"But he's quiet. He doesn't bark or growl or snarl."

"All a burglar would have to do is see him. C'mon, let's go."

Duz finished the last nine cents of his bone. Then the three of us left the yard.

We went door to door. "Would you like to hire...?" I began.

I never got to finish the sentence.

We got two shrieks.

Four gasps.

We got a lady who pulled Pamela and me into the house. And left Duz standing outside. "Now you're safe!" she said.

We got five "Does he bite?"

But nobody waited for an answer.

SLAM!

That was the end of *that*.

And every day I got poorer.

A bag of kibble saved my life.

Well, not exactly. But it gave me hope. It happened a few days after Pamela and I went door to door.

I bought the bag for $4.32. I dropped eighteen cents of it into Duz's three-dollar bowl.

I was thinking my regular thoughts.

How I was going to be this really poor person all my life. How every time I got money for my birthday it would go for kibble.

I started to put the bag away.

Then I saw something on the bag. A picture of a dog. Not just any dog.

It was Genghis Khan, the movie-star dog.

He was big. And mean. And famous. The roughest, toughest dog in Hollywood.

There was a lot of print under his picture. It was about a contest.

In big letters it said: THE GREAT GENGHIS KHAN LOOK-ALIKE CONTEST.

It said they needed a new Genghis Khan. It said this dog wasn't going to be Genghis anymore. He was going to retire.

I liked what I read: YOUR DOG COULD BE A MOVIE STAR FOR A YEAR!

YOUR DOG COULD BE THE NEW GENGHIS KHAN.

DOES YOUR DOG LOOK LIKE GENGHIS?

IF SO, ENTER YOUR DOG NOW!

I stared at Genghis's picture.
He reminded me of someone I knew.
Someone who cost a lot of money.

Someone *who needed a job!*

"Duz Shedd," I said, "how would you like to change your name? How would you like to be the next Genghis Khan?"

Duz raised *both* ears.

Here were the rules.

I had to send in my name, address, and telephone number.

I had to send the dog's name.

I had to tell them how old the dog was. If I knew. I didn't.

I had to tell them how much he weighed. I knew. Too much. All that food.

I had to send a photo of the dog.

Size 8 x 10.

I had to send in everything by the end of the month.

There was more to the contest.

FIRST, WE WILL JUDGE THE PHOTOS.

THEN, IF YOUR DOG LOOKS LIKE GENGHIS, WE WILL FLY THE DOG AND THE DOG'S FAMILY TO OUR GROWL AUDITION IN LOS ANGELES, CALIFORNIA. DOES YOUR DOG HAVE THAT FAMOUS GENGHIS GROWL?

THE WINNER BECOMES GENGHIS KHAN FOR ONE YEAR.

IS YOUR DOG READY FOR HOLLYWOOD?

I was ready for Hollywood.

My money problems would be over.

But what was the Genghis Growl?

Duz never growled.

I couldn't think about that right now. First I had to get a great picture of Duz.

I called Pamela. "Come over," I said. "And bring a camera."

Pamela came over right away. And she

brought her camera. What a friend!

I showed her the bag of kibble.

I pointed to the contest.

"Wow!" she said. "*This* has possibilities." Pamela circled Duz. "But he needs some fixing."

"Fixing?"

"Yeah. A hairdo. A fur-do. Whatever it's called for dogs."

I circled Duz.

I wasn't sure. Duz wasn't sure. He didn't raise an ear.

Pamela grabbed him. She looked at him like he was a person.

"Duz, my friend," she said, "your fur clumps are all wrong. They're not like Genghis's clumps."

Duz's tail went down.

"Don't speak to Duz in a sad voice," I said. "He thinks he did something bad."

Pamela looked Duz in the eye. "You're a good dog, an excellent dog, get it?"

Duz got it. Up went his tail and his ear.

"Scissors, please," Pamela said.

I got a pair of scissors.

"See Genghis's picture," Pamela said. "See where his fur goes up. And his fur goes down. Now watch!"

Pamela started to cut. Snip. Snip.

I closed my eyes. What was she *doing* to Duz?

"Look!" she said. "A *perfect* match!"

I opened my eyes. She was right. Duz went up and down in all the right places.

"Great!" I said. "Now take a nice, mean picture of him."

Pamela pointed to Duz. "You want those big ugly teeth to gleam? Those mean eyes to glare? Those claws to *claw?*"

"Yes. All of the above."

"You need lights. You need poses. You need a real photographer."

I needed money. Again.

I found FINKLE'S FOTOS in the Yellow Pages. Their ad said, WE SNAP PETS AND PEOPLE.

I called them up. "I want you to take my dog's picture," I said.

"Fine," said the voice on the line. "We do dogs. As long as they don't bite. Ha-ha."

"My dog is gentle," I said. "He doesn't even growl."

"Good to hear. Can you come at three tomorrow?"

"Yes. But how much does an 8 x 10 picture cost?"

"It depends. When you come in, we'll talk. And bring a grownup."

I brought my father. He had a day off from work. And he had something even better. He had money.

We walked into FINKLE'S FOTOS. The secretary looked straight at Duz. Then she scurried behind her desk.

"Does he...?" she began.

"He doesn't," I said.

She straightened up.

Dad, Duz, and I waited for the photographer.

"Thanks for coming with me, Dad," I said. "I bet you don't think Duz has any chance of getting to be the new Genghis."

"Well, this is a national contest, Fred. There are lots of mean-looking dogs all over the country."

"I guess so."

"But," said my father, "in my opinion, none of them could look as mean as our Duz."

That cheered me up. I felt good while I waited. Finally the lady said, "You can go in now."

The photographer stared at Duz.

"Cute," he said.

Liar, I thought. But brave.

He pointed to some stuff piled in a corner. "Would you like a bow on your dog? Or a little bell? Want his fur fluffed?"

"Don't touch his fur!" I yelled. "It's clumped just right. Up where it should be up. Down where it should be down."

"Huh?"

"No bows. No bells. I don't want cute. I want mean."

The photographer sighed. "Look, kid. I do man's best friend. Not man's worst enemy."

"Well, forget cute," my father said. "Not all dogs are cute. Not all people are cute. It is not necessary to be cute!"

"But..." the photographer said.

"GRRrrrrr. Do you hear that?" my father said. "That's a growl. We want this dog to look like he's growling."

"Well, it would help if *he* growled and not *you*," the photographer said.

"GRRRrrrrrrrr!!!"

This time my father was not growling. It was Duz. He looked the meanest I had ever seen.

"Quick! Take his picture!" I yelled.

The photographer was in the corner. He had his clipboard held up like a shield.

"*Mean* is not what I do best," he said. "Why don't you try SAFARI SNAPPERS down the street? They've done stampeding elephants, raging rhinos..."

Dad, Duz, and I walked out.

"All we need is one good, mean picture," Pamela said.

She snapped thirty-six.

Duz wouldn't growl for her.

But he showed his teeth. And eyes. And claws.

We took the film to the drugstore.

They had next-day service. It felt like next-year service. It was hard to wait.

Pamela and I were there right after school the next day to pick up the pictures. "Oh, please, please, let there be a good one," she said.

Some of the pictures came out fuzzy.

One had an ear cut off.

One had closed eyes.

Three of them didn't show the clumps clearly.

One of them looked cute. How could that be?

Suddenly Pamela shouted, "This one!" The picture was clear and sharp. It had teeth and clumps and claws and eyes. It was mean. It was great!

"You did it!" I said.

Pamela waved the picture at the man behind the counter. "We need an 8 x 10 of this," she said.

The man looked at the picture. "Are you trying to scare somebody?" He laughed.

"The entire country," Pamela said. She gave the man the negative of the picture. He put it in an envelope.

What if he lost it?

Why was I so scared? All I could think about was that contest. What could go wrong. How we could lose.

That night I had a dream that all the dogs in the state of Nebraska looked mean. Every single one of them.

And they all entered the contest.

I don't live in Nebraska. Or even near.

Would I dream about a different state every night? Would every mean-looking dog in the country show up in my dreams?

No.

The next night I had a new dream.

It was worse than the Nebraska nightmare.

Duz was kissed by a princess. The kiss turned him into a beautiful dog. I asked the princess to turn him back.

She said, "Pay me."

I woke up itchy.

I entered Duz in the contest. Officially.

The 8 x 10 picture came out terrific. And I did all the other stuff I had to do to obey the rules.

Pamela was with me when I went to the post office to mail the envelope. There was a long line. But when people saw Duz, they cleared the way.

As we left the post office, Pamela said, "Now we'll just wait for the news that Duz has won."

"How can you be so sure he's going to win?" I asked.

"I just look at Duz and I believe," she said.

"Have you ever been to Nebraska?" I asked.

"No. Why?"

"Never mind. I just bet that every mean-looking dog in the country is entered in this contest."

Pamela sighed. "Listen, if you saw some of the competition, you would have faith in Duz," she said.

"What do you mean?"

"Well, Dipsey Johnson entered his poodle, Sissy. And Rhoda and Joe McWein entered their teeny tiny dachshund!"

"Are you kidding?"

"No. They say that Genghis Khan is really a tiny dog. And that the movie people dress him up in a big fur coat. And he has false fangs. And a pasted-on tail."

Pamela and I laughed. But down deep I was almost sorry I had entered Duz in the contest. I hated to hope for something that wasn't going to happen.

Weeks went by. Duz's appetite got bigger. And so did the amount of money I owed my mother and father.

One day when I got home from school, my mother stuck an envelope in my hand. "A letter for you," she said.

The envelope had the initials G. K. and an address and a picture of a dog dish in the upper-left-hand corner.

It was from the contest people! I tore open the envelope fast.

There was a letter inside.

DEAR GENGHIS KHAN FAN,

YOUR ENTRY IS AMONG THOSE THAT PASSED OUR FIRST TEST. HOWEVER, WE NEED AN ADDITIONAL PHOTOGRAPH OF

YOUR DOG. THE PHOTO YOU SENT WAS INSUFFICIENT FOR ONE OR MORE OF THE FOLLOWING REASONS:

- ❑ NEEDS TO SHOW FULL FACE
- ❑ NEEDS TO SHOW BOTH EARS
- ❑ NEEDS TO SHOW ALL PAWS
- ☑ NEEDS TO SHOW FULL TAIL
- ❑ NEEDS TO SHOW ALL TEETH

Tail was checked.

I looked at my mother. "Should I be happy about this or not? I think this letter was done on a computer. So they must be sending out lots of them."

My mother shrugged.

I went to my room and got a copy of the photo I had sent in. Sure enough, Duz was sitting on part of his tail.

I called Pamela. "Quick!" I said. "Bring your camera. We need a tail."

"I'll be right over," she said. She didn't even ask me what I meant.

The minute she got to my house, I showed her the letter.

"*What?*" she said. "They are *so* fussy. But this means they are *serious* about Duz."

"You can't be sure."

Pamela grinned. "Well, after you called me, I called Dipsey Johnson and Rhoda and Joe McWein. I asked them if *they* needed a tail."

"And?"

"And they said they didn't know what I was talking about. Actually *I* didn't know what I was talking about. But I figured you had heard from the contest people. And they sure hadn't."

"Maybe their pictures were perfect, and that's why they didn't get a letter."

“Oh, be quiet. Duz is practically a Hollywood star. I love Hollywood. Been there three times.”

Pamela was waving her camera around. I was beginning to get a little excited about this tail request.

But Duz wasn’t.

Pamela aimed her camera at him. But

Duz kept sitting on his tail. We tried to pull it out. Duz sat down harder.

Pamela gave Duz a pep talk. "Now, Duz, you can do this for us. You can do this for *yourself*. You need this job."

Duz kind of yawned.

Finally, thirty-five cents' worth of kibble coaxed Duz into the right pose.

Pamela snapped a whole roll of pictures. Then it was back to the drugstore and the one-day wait.

Success! The next day we had so many terrific pictures that we couldn't pick just one. We sent in a bunch. I hoped that wasn't against the rules.

Now I was back to waiting.

Waiting...waiting...waiting.

Six weeks after I sent in the tails, a special-delivery letter arrived at my house. For me!

My mother watched me open the envelope. She had a look on her face. Like Duz has when he sees a big juicy bone.

I was in such a hurry to open the envelope that I tore part of the letter inside. The letter said:

CONGRATULATIONS! YOUR DOG, DUZ SHEDD, HAS BEEN NAMED A FINALIST IN THE GREAT GENGHIS KHAN LOOK-ALIKE CONTEST!!

YOUR DOG CAN NOW PARTICIPATE IN THE GROWL-A-THON.

THIS IS THE AUDITION TO DETERMINE IF YOUR DOG HAS THAT FAMOUS GENGHIS GROWL.

YOU AND YOUR FAMILY AND YOUR DOG WILL BE FLOWN FIRST-CLASS TO LOS ANGELES, CALIFORNIA, FOR THE AUDITION.

WE WILL PAY ALL EXPENSES FOR YOUR TWO-DAY VISIT. DETAILS TO FOLLOW.

My mother yelled, "Duz is a finalist! We're going to California!"

"Mom," I said. "*I'm* the one who's supposed to yell. I'm the kid, you're the grownup."

Mom and I yelled together.

Suddenly we stopped at the same time. "That Genghis *Growl?*" we said.

"There was something in the rules about it," I said. "Like Genghis has this certain growl. And the winner has to have it too."

Mom sighed. "First the tail, now the growl. It isn't easy getting a job."

We called my father. We called Pamela. They were both excited.

Pamela came running over. She brought something. "Here's a video of Genghis's latest movie, *Genghis Conquers the Aliens*. Let's play it. Let's listen to those growls!"

Pamela, my mother, and I watched together. And listened. My mother even took growl notes.

Genghis was something to watch! Mean, tough, rough.

Duz slept through the movie.

"Now what?" my mother asked. "Duz

is such a peaceful dog. How are we going to get him to growl?"

We all looked at Duz. He was still asleep. No answers there.

"The Genghis Growl is a really big growl," Pamela said.

"GRrrrrr," I said to Duz.

He woke up and wagged his tail.

"Let me try it," Pamela said.

"GRRRRRRRrrrrr!!!"

Duz kept wagging.

"What happens when he sees other dogs?" my mother asked. "Does he growl?"

"No," I said. "He wags."

"What if we gave him a bone and then grabbed it away?" Pamela asked. "I know it's not nice, but..."

"Won't work," my mother said. "Once we took away a bone that had fleas on it. Duz just looked surprised, that's all."

"We have a major problem," Pamela said. "We've just lost the contest."

I was thinking. I was remembering something. About growls. And Duz.

"Wait a minute, wait a minute!" I said. "We've got a chance. But we have to wait until Dad gets home."

"Me?" my father asked. "Me, growl before some judges, and who knows how many other people?"

"You growled for the photographer," I said. "And that made Duz growl. You've got the magic growl to make him growl."

"The photographer...well, that just sort of happened. But a *planned* growl in front of people..."

My mother stared at my father. "It comes down to this, dear. Will you or won't you growl for your son?"

"Well, when you put it that way..."

We had a deal.

"Dad," I said, "growl right now. Let's make sure this plan works."

"GRrrrrrr!" said my father.

Duz looked at my father. He just looked.

But then he opened his jaws. He showed his teeth. "GRRRRRrrrrrr!" Duz answered.

"Let's pack for California," my mother said.

We were flying above the clouds. In an airplane. In first class.

Mom, Dad, me. And Duz.

Duz was snuggled in his seat belt. His chin was on the armrest. We were lucky the seats were wide.

The flight attendant seemed puzzled. "I was told that this dog is some kind of contest finalist," she said. "And he's allowed up here, and he gets our very best."

She served Duz a steak on a beautiful silver plate with a napkin.

"Aren't you scared of our dog?" I asked the attendant.

"No," she said. "Actually he's kind of cute." She scratched Duz's ear.

"Cute?" my father muttered. *"Cute?* We're doomed."

The attendant wiped Duz's mouth with the napkin. "Would you like a pillow and a blanket, sweetie pie?" she asked him.

"Sweetie pie?" my mother gasped.

"This dog doesn't look like a sweetie pie. He looks mean. MEAN!!!"

Things were not going well. But wait till we reach Los Angeles, I thought. Duz would scare the pants off the entire city.

The plane landed.

The taxi driver at the airport, the doorman at the hotel, and the desk clerk all smiled at Duz. Nobody quivered.

"We're doomed," my father repeated.

"I'm so depressed," my mother said. "Duz isn't terrifying *anybody*."

"Aren't they paid to be polite?" I asked. "I bet they were shaking inside."

We went to bed early. Duz had his own dog bed. It was fun going to sleep in a fancy hotel in a big city. But scary too. Because tomorrow was the big test.

The Growl-a-thon was being held at a theater. There was a long, long line of people waiting to get inside.

"Duz is going to have a big audience!" my mother said.

"Oh no," said my father. "I'll be growling in front of half the world!"

Suddenly a man came from nowhere, looked at Duz, and said to us, "Your dog is a finalist? Come with me."

He took us inside through a special door. "Finalists sit in the first three rows.

They're roped off," he said. "We want the dogs away from the audience."

The man chuckled and left.

The roped-off section was empty.

"Looks like we're the first finalists to get here," my father said. "Shall we go sit down?"

Before I could answer, a card was thrust in front of my face. A man was holding it. He said, "Zero Fogg, agent. Genghis is my client. Congrats, kid, on your dog being a finalist. If he wins, he'll need an agent. I represent animals. No humans."

The man kept talking. "Right now I've got a pig with a great future, and an alligator who can play the piano with his jaws, et cetera, et cetera."

"Really?" I said.

"Sure. I made Genghis what he is today. But a year on this job is just enough for any canine. That's why we've started this annual contest."

"Is Genghis pooped?" I asked.

"Well, he's ready to retire. He's going to live on a farm with my sister. My clients get the best."

My father took the card. "We'll think about it," he said.

We made our way to the velvet seats in the front row. Duz sat on the floor. I looked up at the stage. The curtains were drawn.

"It's lonely here," I said. "Maybe Duz is the only finalist."

"No such luck," my mother said. "Here comes some competition."

Two ladies walked in with the meanest-looking dog I have ever seen. Up until then, it was Duz. But this dog looked even meaner than Genghis.

And he made Duz look like a pussycat.

STAGE 1
FOGG

"I told you we're doomed," my father said. "That dog is a true monster!"

Zero Fogg rushed up to the ladies, handed them a card, talked nonstop for five minutes, and walked away.

I went up to the ladies. "How was your trip from Nebraska?" I asked.

"How did you know we're from Nebraska?" one of them asked.

My nightmare was coming true. I looked around for the princess who was going to kiss Duz and make him beautiful.

"I'm Liz and she's Lily," one of the ladies said. "And we'd love to meet your dog."

They were both smiling, but I wasn't sure I trusted them.

"C'mon," I said.

"C'mon, Kong," they said.

"Kong? Your dog is named Kong?"

"Until he becomes Genghis," Lily said sweetly.

We started walking toward my parents and Duz. Kong had a strange walk. More of a stagger.

"Kong is a bit tired from the trip," Liz said. "And he missed his morning nap."

My parents cringed when they saw Kong up close.

I don't know if they were scared of Kong or scared he would win. Or both.

Kong growled at Duz. It was a deep, strong growl. Duz wagged his tail.

"Oh, what an adorable dog you have," Lily oozed.

"A real kitchy-coo," Liz purred.

Liz and Lily looked at each other slyly.

I was mad! "My dog is *scary*, get it?" I said. "He is not a kitchy-coo. If the flight attendant and the taxi driver and the door-man and the desk clerk don't act scared, well, maybe they're just polite."

I took a deep breath. "But you! You *hope* he's adorable. Well, he's not!"

These ladies were not nice. More than ever I hoped their dog would lose.

They walked away.

Kong followed. He seemed to be sleeping while he walked.

Just then another dog and its owner arrived. The owner was full of muscles. He wore a bandanna and a leather jacket.

His dog looked exactly like Duz.

Only bigger.

Zero Fogg came running after the man. He was waving his card. "Stop!" Zero said. "I hold your dog's future in my hands."

The man didn't stop. He and his dog walked toward us. The dog growled at Duz.

I already knew it would be a deep, strong growl. Duz wagged his tail.

The man grinned. "This is an attack dog, but don't worry. Nice to meet you. May the best dog win."

The man walked over to Liz, Lily, and Kong.

"We're not just doomed," my father said. "We're dead."

Mom, Dad, and I kept watching the door for new contestants. Nobody else came. At last my mother said, "There are only two other finalists!"

"Yeah, but look at them," I said. "And listen to them."

Suddenly there was a loud noise. Doors swung open and people poured into the theater. The crowd from outside was coming in. And I saw TV cameras. And people who looked like reporters.

Everyone settled into their seats. The stage curtains opened.

Up on the stage were two men, a woman, and…in person…Genghis Khan!

Genghis was sitting on a kind of throne made of pillows.

There was a huge banner hanging across the stage: THE GREAT GENGHIS KHAN GROWL-A-THON!

And there was a microphone.

The woman stepped up to the mike. "Welcome, finalists," she said. "This is it. The event you've been growling for."

She gave a little laugh.

"Just remember, even if your dog doesn't win, you're all still winners. Did we enjoy that all-expenses-paid trip to Los Angeles or what?"

Mom, Dad, and I and Liz and Lily applauded. The muscleman hollered, "I *live* in Los Angeles!"

The woman went on. "Let me introduce myself. I'm Ms. Crunch. I represent your favorite dog-food company, and we all know what that is."

She waited for applause. Then she said, "Mr. Swaggs, on my left, represents Slambang Entertainment, the company that made Genghis Khan a star. The man on my right is Genghis's agent, Zero Fogg.

"Now, we have scientifically picked the order of the dogs' auditions. The first dog to come up is Slash. Sir?"

The muscleman said, "Go, Slash!"

Slash bounded up to the stage. He went right up to Genghis. He growled, "GRRRRRRRRRRrrrr!" Just like that. No coaching. Nothing.

Genghis growled back. It wasn't anything special. Just a growl. Genghis seemed bored.

"Excellent, Slash," said Ms. Crunch.

The muscleman put his fingers between his teeth and whistled. Slash leaped from the stage.

"Next," said Ms. Crunch.

I was shaking. Would it be Kong or Duz? Did it matter? Already Slash had done a world-class growl.

"Kong!" Ms. Crunch called.

Then she called again. "Kong, do you hear me?"

I looked at Liz and Lily. They were bent over Kong. He was fast asleep. He was snoring.

"Wake up, wake up, you idiot mutt," they were yelling. They were tugging too. The poor dog was getting pushed and pulled. But he just snored louder.

Nothing could wake mighty Kong.

"Nuts!" the ladies said.

Ms. Crunch sighed. "I'm terribly afraid that Kong is disqualified," she said. "Sleepyheads simply don't make good movie stars. Next! Duz?"

Dad stood up. "C'mon, Duz," he said. Dad and Duz walked toward the stage.

"Oh, dear," said Ms. Crunch. "No humans are allowed with the dogs. It's the dog's audition."

THE GREAT GENGHIS KHAN GROWL-A-THON!
ZZZZZZZZZZZZ

"But I just need to growl once," my father said. "It inspires Duz to growl."

"Oh, we can't have that," Ms. Crunch said. "These dogs must growl on their own! We will train the winner for the movies, but first he needs a *natural* talent."

My father slunk back to his seat.

My mother held my hand. My dream died.

There was total silence. Duz was on the stage. He just stood there. It was his turn to growl. I knew he wouldn't.

Slowly he walked up to Genghis and sniffed. Genghis got up from his throne. He sniffed back.

Then Genghis bared his teeth. And he growled. "GRRRRRRRRRRRRRRRrrrrr!!!!!"

It was ear-splitting.

Then I heard it again. Louder.

"GRRRRRRRRRRRRRRRRRRRRRrrrr!!!!!"

This dog was amazing!

But wait a minute! Genghis hadn't

growled again. The second growl came from *Duz!*

Sure enough. Ms. Crunch was pointing to Duz. Duz and Genghis had exchanged growls!

But now they were circling each other. And sniffing. They were getting ready for a fight. I just knew it.

I ran up to the stage to separate them.

I got a good closeup look at Genghis. I looked him all over.

"I don't believe this!" I said to myself. Genghis wasn't a *he*. Genghis Khan was a *girl!*

Now she and Duz were nose to nose. They kept staring at each other. Genghis and Duz were falling in love. Or something like that. Those growls must have been love growls.

Zero Fogg came over and grabbed Genghis. "Just *sit*, boy."

"She's a girl," I said. "And she's sweet, just like my Duz. She only looks mean, just like my Duz."

"Young man, you may return to your seat," Ms. Crunch said. "And take Duz with you."

I had just wrecked everything. Why couldn't I have kept quiet! Now Duz would never be Genghis. Now I would owe my parents money forever. Just before I left for California, I looked at my total again. $248.10. And it would only get bigger.

Ms. Crunch announced, "Mr. Swaggs, Mr. Fogg, and I will now pick the winner."

My parents hugged Duz and me. Then

they clutched my arms while Ms. Crunch, Mr. Swaggs, and Zero Fogg whispered together. It seemed like they whispered for five years.

Then Ms. Crunch went up to the mike. "We have picked a winner. Our new Genghis Khan is...........DUZ SHEDD!!!"

I couldn't believe it!! My parents and I leaped up from our seats. My dad was so happy he had tears in his eyes.

The muscleman shouted, "For this I had to miss a morning at the gym!" And he stomped out with Slash.

Liz and Lily were still trying to wake Kong.

Ms. Crunch called out, "Now, will our winner please come up here and bring his family!"

Flashbulbs popped while we walked.

Ms. Crunch patted Duz. Then her voice

boomed out. "Duz Shedd, you have won a movie contract for a year! And a beautiful home for you and your family to stay in." She smiled at the audience. "Now let's give the Shedds a warm, Hollywood welcome!"

There was applause. And screaming. Then people started crowding onto the stage. Grownups. Kids. "Autograph! Autograph!" they shouted.

I began to sign.

"Pawprint!" somebody said. "I want your dog's print!"

I knew that voice! I looked up.

Pamela was there!

I hugged her hard.

"I talked my folks into coming," she said. "I didn't want to tell you in case Duz...uh..."

"Lost?" I said.

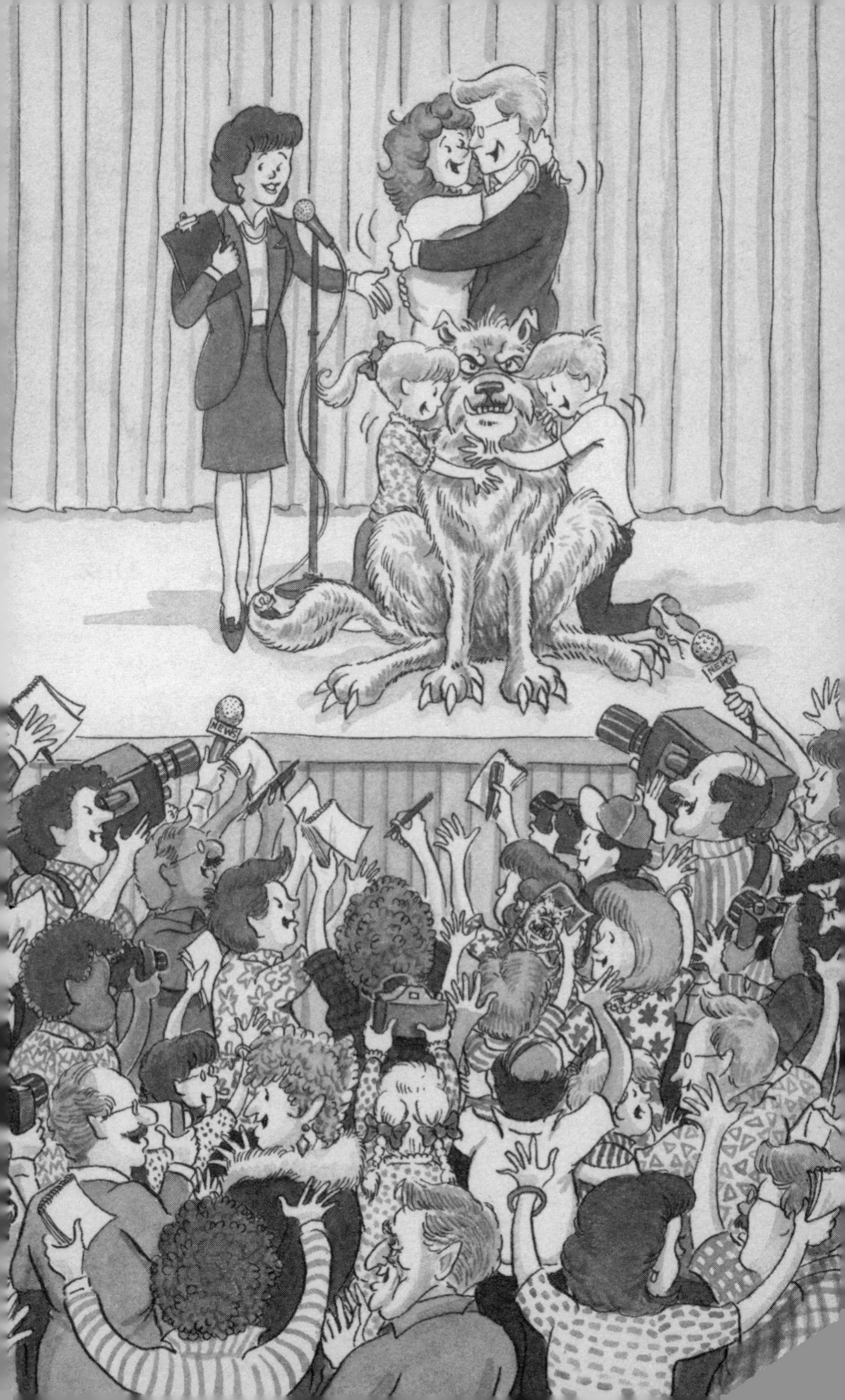
NEWS
NEWS

"Yeah. I'd be here to cheer you up. But he won! He won! He won!"

Pamela was dancing.

TV cameramen zoomed in on us. And on Duz. And my parents. There were more flashbulbs popping. This was it!

I was staring at Duz. An ear went up. Then the other. Then the tail went into motion. I guess he really liked being Duz Shedd Genghis Khan or the other way around.

Hollywood. A year's contract with a movie studio. Stardom. Suddenly it was real!

My father would have to give up his job. My mother didn't have a job to give up.

I would have to change schools.

I wouldn't see Pamela every day. Or even every week. But I knew she'd visit.

And it was only for a year.

A year when my dog would become rich and famous. And maybe get married.

I wanted it more than I had ever wanted anything.

But I had one question.

I turned to Ms. Crunch. “Exactly how long will it take for Duz to earn $248.10?”

Don't miss the next Genghis Khan book!

"My name is Fritz," the man said. "I have a limo for you."

We settled back in a beautiful silver car. "My first limo," my mother sighed.

We drove through neighborhoods with huge homes and big trees. At last we turned up a long, winding path. We stopped in front of a house that looked like it belonged to a...well...a movie star!

There were three acres. And palm trees. And a swimming pool. Awesome!

"This is *ours?*" my father said.

"Your home sweet home for a year," Fritz told us.

From *Genghis Khan, A Star Is Born!*
by Marjorie Weinman Sharmat

MARJORIE WEINMAN SHARMAT is best known for creating super-sleuth Nate the Great. Her books have been translated into fourteen languages and have won numerous awards. She insists that Duz is not based on her dog, Dudley—who, she says, is "definitely cute" and only bites on Tuesdays.

Ms. Sharmat lives with her husband, Mitchell. They have two sons—Craig and Andrew—and a new grandson, Nathan.